Horse Shoes

Nancy Tuminelly

Illustrated by C.A. Nobens

Consulting Editor, Diane Craig, M.A./Reading Specialist

ABDO
Publishing Company

Published by ABDO Publishing Company, 4940 Viking Drive, Edina, Minnesota 55435.

Printed in the United States.

Credits
Edited by: Pam Price
Curriculum Coordinator: Nancy Tuminelly
Cover and Interior Design and Production: Mighty Media
Photo Credits: AbleStock, Corel, Photodisc, ShutterStock

Library of Congress Cataloging-in-Publication Data

Tuminelly, Nancy, 1952-
    Horse shoes / Nancy Tuminelly ; illustrated by C.A. Nobens.
      p. cm. -- (Fact & fiction. Animal tales)
    Summary: Frannie Foal is nervous about starting school, so her mother pampers her with special treats, including a new pair of saddle shoes. Includes facts about horses.
    Includes index.
    ISBN 1-59679-943-9 (hardcover)
    ISBN 1-59679-944-7 (paperback)
    [1. Mothers and daughters--Fiction. 2. Individuality--Fiction. 3. Horses--Fiction.] I. Nobens, C.A., ill.
  II. Title. III. Series.

    PZ7.T82326Hor 2006
    [E]--dc22

                                                                                    2005024468

SandCastle Level: Fluent

SandCastle™ books are created by a professional team of educators, reading specialists, and content developers around five essential components—phonemic awareness, phonics, vocabulary, text comprehension, and fluency—to assist young readers as they develop reading skills and strategies and increase their general knowledge. All books are written, reviewed, and leveled for guided reading, early reading intervention, and Accelerated Reader® programs for use in shared, guided, and independent reading and writing activities to support a balanced approach to literacy instruction. The SandCastle™ series has four levels that correspond to early literacy development. The levels help teachers and parents select appropriate books for young readers.

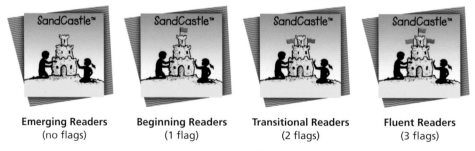

Emerging Readers	Beginning Readers	Transitional Readers	Fluent Readers
(no flags)	(1 flag)	(2 flags)	(3 flags)

These levels are meant only as a guide. All levels are subject to change.

FACT & FICTION

This series provides early fluent readers the opportunity to develop reading comprehension strategies and increase fluency. These books are appropriate for guided, shared, and independent reading.

FACT The left-hand pages incorporate realistic photographs to enhance readers' understanding of informational text.

FICTION The right-hand pages engage readers with an entertaining, narrative story that is supported by whimsical illustrations.

The Fact and Fiction pages can be read separately to improve comprehension through questioning, predicting, making inferences, and summarizing. They can also be read side-by-side, in spreads, which encourages students to explore and examine different writing styles.

FACT OR FICTION? This fun quiz helps reinforce students' understanding of what is real and not real.

SPEED READ The text-only version of each section includes word-count rulers for fluency practice and assessment.

GLOSSARY Higher-level vocabulary and concepts are defined in the glossary.

SandCastle™ would like to hear from you.

Tell us your stories about reading this book. What was your favorite page? Was there something hard that you needed help with? Share the ups and downs of learning to read. To get posted on the ABDO Publishing Company Web site, send us an e-mail at:

sandcastle@abdopublishing.com

A female horse is called a mare. A baby horse is called a foal.

Tomorrow is the first day of school. Frannie Foal says to Mama Mare, "I don't want to go to school! I'm afraid that no one will be my friend."

5

The hair on a horse's neck is called a mane. Some manes are long. Some manes are short.

Frannie looks at herself in the pond and says, "If I braid my hair and dye it purple, everyone will think I'm cool and will want to be my friend."

7

Horses can see in two directions at once. But horses cannot see right in front of them.

"If I wear big purple-glitter glasses, then I'll look hip and everyone will like me," Frannie says.

Horses use their tails to swat flies. Horses also swish their tails to communicate with other horses.

Mama swishes her tail and says, "Have fun with what you look like and what you wear! But others will like you and want to be your friend for who you are. Just be yourself, Frannie."

Frannie thinks for a moment. "I guess you're right," she says.

11

Horses eat grass, oats, and hay. Horses eat carrots and apples too.

"I'm hungry! May I have a burger and fries for lunch?" Frannie asks.

"Okay," Mama says, "but it's veggie soup for dinner!" They gallop back to the barn.

Horses have many kinds of markings. One marking looks like socks.

14

"Your shoes do look small," Mama says. "After lunch, we'll go shopping. Maybe we can find some shoes that will be fun to wear with your favorite socks."

15

Horses' hooves grow like toenails and must be cleaned and trimmed. Many horses wear metal shoes to protect their hooves.

They go to five stores before Frannie finds the perfect shoes.

Frannie exclaims, "These are really me!" as she prances around in blue-and-orange high-heeled saddle shoes. "They look great with my orange polka-dot knee-highs!"

17

Horses do not like people to pat them.
Horses like to be rubbed and stroked
instead.

That night, Mama tucks Frannie into bed and rubs her back. "I'm excited to go to school tomorrow. I hope we have burgers and fries for lunch," Frannie says as she closes her eyes. "And thank you, Mama, for the new shoes!"

19

FACT OR FiCTioN?

Read each statement below. Then decide whether it's from the FACT section or the FiCTioN section!

1. Horses use their tails to swat flies.

2. Horses can see in two directions at once.

3. Horses go to stores to shop for shoes.

4. Horses eat burgers and fries.

ANSWERS
1. fact 2. fact 3. fiction 4. fiction

A female horse is called a mare. A baby horse is
called a foal.

The hair on a horse's neck is called a mane. Some
manes are long. Some manes are short.

Horses can see in two directions at once. But horses
cannot see right in front of them.

Horses use their tails to swat flies. Horses also swish
their tails to communicate with other horses.

Horses eat grass, oats, and hay. Horses eat carrots
and apples too.

Horses have many kinds of markings. One marking
looks like socks.

Horses' hooves grow like toenails and must be
cleaned and trimmed. Many horses wear metal shoes
to protect their hooves.

Horses do not like people to pat them. Horses like
to be rubbed and stroked instead.

Tomorrow is the first day of school. Frannie 8

Foal says to Mama Mare, "I don't want to go to 19

school! I'm afraid that no one will be my friend." 29

Frannie looks at herself in the pond and says, 38

"If I braid my hair and dye it purple, everyone 48

will think I'm cool and will want to be my 58

friend." 59

"If I wear big purple-glitter glasses, then I'll look 69

hip and everyone will like me," Frannie says. 77

Mama swishes her tail and says, "Have fun 85

with what you look like and what you wear! But 95

others will like you and want to be your friend 105

for who you are. Just be yourself, Frannie." 113

Frannie thinks for a moment. "I guess you're 121

right," she says. 124

"I'm hungry! May I have a burger and fries for 134

lunch?" Frannie asks. 137

"Okay," Mama says, "but it's veggie soup for 145

dinner!" They gallop back to the barn. 152

22

"Your shoes do look small," Mama says. "After lunch, we'll go shopping. Maybe we can find some shoes that will be fun to wear with your favorite socks."

They go to five stores before Frannie finds the perfect shoes.

Frannie exclaims, "These are really me!" as she prances around in blue-and-orange high-heeled saddle shoes. "They look great with my orange polka-dot knee-highs!"

That night, Mama tucks Frannie into bed and rubs her back. "I'm excited to go to school tomorrow. I hope we have burgers and fries for lunch," Frannie says as she closes her eyes. "And thank you, Mama, for the new shoes!"

GLOSSARY

hoof. the hard covering that protects the foot of an animal such as a horse, cow, or deer

knee-high. a sock or stocking that covers the foot and leg up to the knee

marking. the usual pattern of color on an animal

pond. a body of water smaller than a lake

prance. to walk in a lively, springy way

saddle shoe. a laced, leather shoe that has a black or colored band of leather across the instep

To see a complete list of SandCastle™ books and other nonfiction titles from ABDO Publishing Company, visit www.abdopublishing.com or contact us at: 4940 Viking Drive, Edina, Minnesota 55435 • 1-800-800-1312 • fax: 1-952-831-1632